Disney · PIXAR

Cars

STORYBOOK COLLECTION

Disney PRESS

New York

TABLE OF CONTENTS

Printed in the United States of America

First Edition

10 9 8 7 6 5 4

ILS No. G942-9090-6-12247

This book is set in 18-point Goudy Infant.

Library of Congress Catalog Card Number on file

ISBN 978-1-4231-2495-5

Visit www.disneybooks.com

SUSTAINABLE FORESTRY INITIATIVE Certified Sourcing www.sfiprogram.org SFI-00993 For Text Only

A New Car in Town

On the day of the biggest race of the year, a rookie named Lightning McQueen was getting ready in his trailer.

"I'm faster than fast. Quicker than quick," he said aloud. "I am Lightning."

Suddenly, he heard a noise at the front of the trailer.

"Hey, Lightning," called Mack. He drove the race car's custom tractor trailer to each race. "You ready?"

The door to the trailer lowered and Lightning zipped out. The sun glinted off his bright red finish, and the crowd went wild as he flashed his lucky lightning-bolt sticker.

"*Ka-chow!*" Lightning exclaimed. He was ready to race.

Lightning was up against a lot of cars—including his biggest rivals, Chick Hicks and The King. They were all competing for the season title and the famous Piston Cup.

The King had won the cup the past few years. Now he was about to retire, and he was determined to win one last time. But Chick wanted to win, too. And so did Lightning.

The flag dropped, and the cars took off around the track. The King was in the lead. Lightning pulled up next to Chick.

Suddenly—SLAM! Chick crashed into Lightning. The rookie skidded off the track. Laughing, Chick slammed into another car and caused a huge wreck.

"Get through that!" he yelled.

The wreck didn't stop Lightning, though. He made a few quick moves and soon passed Chick and The King on the straightaway. Lightning was in the lead!

When he made a pit stop, Lightning's pit crew told him he needed new tires. But the race car wouldn't listen. "No tires, just gas!" said Lightning.

Back on the track, Lightning was in the lead with only one lap to go when—BANG! BANG! He blew both rear tires!

Chick and The King quickly caught up to him at the finish line. Lightning stuck out his tongue as they crossed, hoping that would make him the winner.

While the cars waited to hear who had won, fans and reporters rushed over to Lightning.

"Are you sorry you didn't have a crew chief out there?" asked one reporter.

"No," said Lightning. "I'm a one-man show."

Lightning's pit crew was upset. They didn't want to work with a car who didn't think he needed a team, so they quit.

"You need to wise up and get yourself a good crew chief and a good team," The King told Lightning.

Suddenly, an announcement came over the loudspeaker: "We have a three-way tie! A tiebreaker race will be held in California in one week."

Lightning wanted to get to California before Chick. Dinoco sponsored The King. Once he retired, the company would need a new car to represent them. Lightning wanted to do it!

He and Mack set off. After driving for a day, Mack needed to rest. Lightning promised to stay awake if they drove all night.

Soon, the race car fell asleep. Then Mack started to doze. He swerved suddenly, and his trailer door opened. Still asleep, Lightning rolled out onto the highway.

Beep! Beep! The race car woke to the sound of cars honking. He realized that he was going the wrong way!

"Mack!" Lightning called. He followed a tractor trailer off the highway. But it wasn't Mack.

Suddenly, he heard a *pop, pop, pop.* He thought someone had shot at him! Lighting raced ahead. He caught his tires on some wires, causing all kinds of damage.

Sheriff, whose tailpipe had backfired, finally caught him.

The next morning, when Lightning woke up, he had a parking boot on one of his tires so he couldn't drive. A rusty old tow truck was smiling at him.

"My name's Mater," said the tow truck. "Like Tuh-mater, but without the 'Tuh.'"

Lightning looked around. "Where am I?" he asked.

"Radiator Springs," said Mater. "The cutest little town in Carburetor County."

Just then, Sheriff pulled up. "Tow this road hazard to traffic court!" he ordered.

When he entered the courtroom, Lightning was met by a group of angry townsfolk. The judge was a gruff blue car named Doc Hudson. As soon as he saw that Lightning was a race car, Doc ordered him out of the court. "I want him out of our town!"

Before Lightning could leave, a beautiful blue sports car named Sally rolled into the courtroom.

"Doc, make this guy fix the road," Sally pleaded. She explained that Radiator Springs wouldn't survive without its main road. The other cars agreed.

Doc changed his mind. He ordered Lightning to repair the pavement.

Doc brought Lightning to Bessie, a giant road-paving machine. When Doc took off Lightning's parking boot, the race car tried to escape. But he didn't get very far. His gas tank was empty.

Mater towed Lightning back to town. The race car began to pull Bessie slowly down the street.

A few hours later, Lightning still had a long way to go. He heard on the radio that Chick Hicks was already in California. That meant Chick would get to Dinoco first!

Lightning couldn't let that happen. He pulled Bessie as fast as he could. Panting, Lightning finally made it to the end.

"I'm finished," he announced. "Just say thank you and I'll be on my way."

"The deal was you fix the road, not make it worse," said Doc. "Start over."

"Look, Grandpa," said Lightning. "I'm not a bulldozer, I'm a race car."

Doc challenged Lightning to a race. "If you win, you go. If I win, you do the road my way," he said.

"Let's race," Lightning said with a laugh. He knew the old car didn't have a chance.

Out on an old dirt road, Lightning revved his engine. When the starting flag dropped, he took off.

Doc Hudson didn't move. He watched as Lightning sped down the track. Then the race car hit a sharp left turn and lost control. He fell over the edge of a cliff and landed in a cactus patch below.

"You drive like you fix roads," Doc called to Lightning, "lousy." Doc left Mater to tow the rookie.

Lightning was furious, but he got back to work. "I'll show him," he muttered.

The next morning, the cars of Radiator Springs woke to the sound of Mater cheering. He was driving circles on a section of smooth, newly-paved road.

"Amazing!" said Sally.

Lightning had done such

a good job that even Doc was impressed. He looked around. Then he heard the roar of a race car in the distance. He found Lightning on the dirt road, practicing his turns.

Doc gave him some advice: turn right to go left.

Lightning laughed. Still, he gave Doc's advice a try. But he went right over the cliff again.

That afternoon, Lightning was back at work on the rest of the road. In fact, he was doing such a good job that all the cars in town started to fix up their shops, too. Sally was thrilled.

Luigi, the owner of the tire shop, wanted to spruce up more than just his shop. He tried to sell Lightning new tires.

The race car was not in the mood, though. "Look, I get all my tires for free," he said. "No, thank you."

Just then, Lightning was hit with a blast of water.

"Stop!" he shouted. He opened his eyes and saw Sally and Red the fire engine in front of him.

"Red, you missed a spot," said Sally. Red sprayed the race car again.

"What was that for?" asked Lightning.

Sally explained that Lightning had to be clean if he wanted to stay at her motel, the Cozy Cone. "I just thought I'd say

thank you for doing a great job," she said.

That night, Mater invited Lightning to go tractor tipping. Together, they drove through a field of sleeping tractors. When they got close to one, Mater honked his horn and the tractor would tip over with a loud moan. Lightning and Mater laughed.

Suddenly, a huge combine came charging toward them!

"Run!" cried Mater. "Frank's gonna catch you!"

Mater took off through the field, laughing. But Lightning was terrified. They made it to a fence and zipped through an opening just in time.

"That was fun," said Mater when they were back in town. He began to drive backward in circles, spinning past Lightning.

"That was incredible!" said Lightning. He realized he was actually having fun with Mater. He was surprised, but happy, too.

"I knew it!" said the tow truck. "I made a good choice."

"In what?" asked Lightning.

"My best friend," answered Mater.

When Lightning pulled into the Cozy Cone Motel that night, Sally drove over to talk to him.

"You know, Mater trusts you," she told him. She was worried that Lightning would let down his new friend when he left.

"Yeah, okay," the race car said. "Look, I'm exhausted. It's been a long day."

Disappointed, Sally turned toward her office.

"Hey," called Lightning. "Thanks for letting me stay here. It's great." He smiled.

Lightning realized he was starting to like Radiator Springs.

A Real Winner

Lightning McQueen had been in Radiator Springs for a few days. He was eager to get to California for his next race, but he was starting to like the little town, too.

One morning, the race car went to see Doc Hudson. Doc was busy, so he told Lightning to wait at Flo's V8 Café.

On his way out of Doc's garage, Lightning peeked inside the back office. He saw a dirty old cup filled with tools. A plaque on it said: HUDSON HORNET—CHAMPION, 1951.

"He has a Piston Cup!" said Lightning. Then he spotted two more. "Three Piston Cups?"

Suddenly, Doc came through the doorway. He was furious. "The sign stays 'stay out.'"

Lightning looked closely at Doc. "You're the Hudson Hornet!" Lightning cried. "You hold the record for most wins in a season. You've got to show me your tricks!"

"I already tried that," said Doc.

"You won the championship three times! Look at those trophies!" Lightning exclaimed.

"All I see is a bunch of empty cups," said Doc angrily. Then he slammed the door in Lightning's face.

Lightning hurried over to Flo's. "Guys!" he called out. "Did you know Doc is a famous race car?"

The other cars looked at each other. Then they burst out laughing.

"Our Doc?" asked Sheriff.

"Are you sick, buddy?" asked Mater.

Lightning's excitement faded as he realized that no one believed him.

Suddenly, Sally drove up. She filled Lightning's gas tank.

"Hey!" cried Sheriff. He was worried Lightning would use the gas to try to leave town again.

"It's okay, Sheriff," said Sally with a smile. "I trust him."

She asked the race car to go for a drive with her.

"Where are we going?" Lightning asked.

"I don't know," answered Sally. Then she took off.

Lightning chased after her. He wasn't used to racing just for fun.

The pair sped past a forest, laughing and joking as they took turns passing each other. They climbed up the side of a mountain and soon came to an abandoned motel.

"Wow," said Lightning. "What is this place?"

"It used to be the most popular stop," said Sally.

She brought Lightning over to a cliff that looked out on a valley. The sun shone on big red mountains, and they could see Radiator Springs down below.

Cars sped through the valley on the highway. They were driving right past Radiator Springs, not even realizing what they were missing.

Sally explained that Radiator Springs had once been a bright, bustling town filled with customers. But then the Interstate was built, and the town slowly lost its business.

"The town got bypassed just to save ten minutes of driving," she said sadly.

That afternoon, Lightning found Doc out on the old dirt track. The race car watched in awe as Doc roared down the track, leaving swirls of dust behind him. Doc came up to the turn that Lightning hadn't been able to make. He had no problem with it!

"You're amazing!" cried Lightning.

Doc didn't say a word. Instead, he turned around and sped away, throwing a cloud of dust at the rookie.

Lightning wanted to know more about Doc's racing days. He followed Doc back to his office.

"How could you quit at the top of your game?" Lightning asked.

"You think *I* quit?" roared Doc. "They quit on me." He showed Lightning an old newspaper clipping about his big crash. By the time Doc was ready to race again,

he had already been replaced by a hotshot rookie.

"I keep that to remind me never to go back," Doc said, pointing to the article. Then he looked at Lightning. "Just finish that road and get out of here!"

The next morning, the cars of Radiator Springs woke to find a road that was so slick and smooth it looked brand-new. Lightning had finished paving it during the night. The cars were happy to have a new road, but they grew sad when they realized that it meant Lightning had left.

Doc didn't seem to mind. "Good riddance," he said.

Just then, Lightning drove up. "I can't go just yet," he told everyone. "I'm not sure these tires can get me all the way to California."

Luigi cheered. He took Lightning to his tire shop, where the race car got four new tires. When Lightning was done at Luigi's, he visited the rest of the shops in town for fuel, stickers, and a fresh paint job.

That night, the shops all turned on their signs and everyone came out to cruise up and down the new road. Radiator Springs was bright and lively again, just like it had been many years before. Lightning had worked with the other cars in town to surprise Sally.

Sally was thrilled. "It's even better than I pictured it," she said to Lightning. "Thank you."

Suddenly, a spotlight shone down on the race car. A helicopter circled overhead.

"We have found Lightning McQueen!" shouted a voice from a loudspeaker.

Photographers and reporters swept into Radiator Springs and crowded around Lightning.

The race car looked for Sally. They had gotten separated.

Just then, Lightning's trailer, Mack, pulled up. He had the race car's agent, Harv, on the phone.

"You've got to get to Cali, pronto!" cried Harv. He told Lightning that Chick Hicks was getting ready to make a deal with Dinoco. Lightning drove over to Sally.

"Good luck in California," she said. "I hope you find what you're looking for."

Before he could respond, Sally pulled away and Mack whisked Lightning out of Radiator Springs.

As the press followed Lightning and Mack out of town, a reporter pulled up next to Doc.

"Thanks for the call," she said to him.

Sally overheard. She looked at Doc Hudson in shock. "You called them?" she asked.

"It's best for everyone," Doc replied.

Sally looked at the rest of the townsfolk. They all looked sad that their new friend was gone. "Best for everyone, or best for you?" Sally said. She turned and headed for her motel.

"I didn't get to say good-bye," said Mater.

Doc started to wonder if he had made a mistake.

The next day, Lightning hit the track to race The King and Chick Hicks for the Piston Cup. But he couldn't stop thinking about his friends in Radiator Springs.

"Speed. I am speed," he said, trying to focus on the race. But he quickly fell behind.

Suddenly, Doc's voice came over Lightning's radio. "I didn't come all this way to see you quit."

Lightning saw Doc, Mater, and some of his new friends from Radiator Springs. They were working as his pit crew!

"You can win this race with your eyes shut," said Doc.

Lightning revved his engine and began to catch up to Chick and The King.

But Chick was a mean racer. He bumped into Lightning. Just as Lightning was about to spin out, he remembered Doc's advice: turn right to go left. He gave it a try. This time it worked—he took the lead!

Lightning was in first place. Chick and The King were fighting for second. Suddenly, Chick hit The King. The older car flipped across the track and crashed into the wall.

Lightning was about to cross the finish line when he saw the crash on a big video screen. Lightning thought of the newspaper clipping about Doc's crash years ago. He slammed on his brakes. Chick sped across the finish line first.

Lightning turned around and drove over to The King.

"I think The King should finish his last race," said Lightning. Then he pushed the old race car back onto the track and all the way across the finish line.

The crowd booed Chick as he accepted his Piston Cup. But they broke out in cheers for Lightning and The King.

"You've got a lot of stuff, kid," said Doc.

Lightning was celebrating with his friends when Tex, the owner of Dinoco, came over to talk to him.

"How would you like to be the new face of Dinoco?" asked Tex.

A few days earlier, Lightning would have jumped at the chance. But now he turned down the offer. He had a sponsor and a pit crew that he liked.

After the race, Lightning drove back to the cliff that overlooked Radiator Springs. He found Sally at the top.

"Just passing through?" she asked him.

"Actually, I thought I'd stay a while," said Lightning.

Sally broke into a huge smile. Lightning smiled, too. "Why don't we take a drive?" he asked.

"*Naaah,*" she answered with a grin. Then she zipped off down the hill.

"*Ka-chow!*" Lightning shouted as he followed right behind her. He was excited to be back in Radiator Springs.

A Place to
Call Home

Lightning McQueen, a hotshot rookie race car, had just finished the most important race of his career. He hadn't come in first, but he had proven he was a car to watch.

Now, he was driving back to his new home in Radiator Springs with his friends. They had all gone to California to cheer him on.

Sheriff pulled up alongside Lightning as they drove. "We're mighty glad you've decided to stay in Radiator Springs," he said.

"Me, too," Lightning said. "I just don't want to spend any more time with Bessie," he joked. Bessie was a paving machine that Lightning had worked with to  repave a portion of the local road he'd torn up.

Sheriff laughed. Then he said, "Bessie is an important member of town, too. Why, without her, our streets would still be dirt!"

Mater pulled up ahead of the other cars. "You can't turn as easy on dirt," he said as he drove in the shape of an eight. "And forget about driving backward! I'm sure glad these roads are so smooth."

"Wow," Lightning said. "I didn't know Bessie had been here that long."

"Son, there's a lot you don't know about this town," Sheriff said. He began to tell Lightning about it.

A car named Stanley had been the first to cruise into the area. He decided to name the town Radiator Springs. When Lizzie rolled in years later, Stanley fell in love and asked her to stay and sell bumper stickers in a curio shop.

At first Lizzie's shop was just a tent at the side of the road. As new cars began to settle in town, Lizzie and Stanley helped them open their own stores. Lizzie even moved into a building in the center of town.

It seemed that just about every car that traveled that way stopped in Radiator Springs. The cars opened a tire shop, a paint shop, and a café, among many other stores. Anything a car wanted could be found in the friendly little town.

Then Sheriff explained how a wealthy and important car from Las Vegas had opened the Wheel Well Motel.

"That was some fancy motel," Sheriff said. "We even had the governor come spend the night. That's when we knew we were a proper town."

Lightning knew about the old motel. Sally had brought him up there to see the valley when he'd first come to Radiator Springs. He knew she'd loved the old building. As Sheriff continued to describe the town, Lightning wished he could have been there to see it then!

"Radiator Springs was the best stop on the mother road," Sheriff said.

"And you were here in town then?" Lightning asked.

"You bet!" Sheriff exclaimed. "With the town growing, I was hired to keep the riffraff under control."

"I hired Red, too," Sheriff continued. He glanced at the shy fire engine at the edge of the crowd of cars. "I knew we needed a firefighter, and Red's about the most helpful truck I know."

The fire engine, who had been listening, blushed.

Sheriff chuckled. "Took some folks a while to realize that even though Red is so shy, he'll always be there when you need him."

45

"Mater rolled into town next," Sheriff continued.

"That's right!" the tow truck interrupted. "I was towing this car who'd blown a gasket, and we heard there was a doctor here in town."

The cars turned to look at Doc Hudson. He sighed, then said, "After my racing days were over, I'd been looking for a town where I could slow down. Couldn't imagine a better place than here," he finished with a small smile.

Lightning listened eagerly as the other cars told their stories. He knew Sally, the shiny blue sports car, had been a lawyer in California. But he had never heard about Luigi's and Guido's boat ride all the way from Italy!

Flo had been a famous show car. She came to Radiator Springs while the Motorama Girls were traveling to their next show. She decided to stay in town after she met Ramone. They'd been cruising low and slow ever since.

"Wow," Lightning said once everyone had told their stories. The cars had made it back to town and were at Flo's V8 Café. After the long trip, they were ready for a sip of oil. "It's great that so many cars stopped here along the way and decided to stay."

The cars looked at one another. "See," Sally finally said, "Radiator Springs still is *the* stop on the mother road." She smiled. "The town just wouldn't be the same if we all hadn't ended up here."

Mater grinned. "I'm sure glad I stayed here. Where would I have opened Tow Mater's if I hadn't?"

Lizzie drove over to welcome everyone back home. "It was so quiet here without you. I started to think I'd have to find new cars to resettle in this town."

" 'Course not," Doc replied. "We took the long road home is all. But it's good to be back."

That night the cars all gathered in town. They thought about going to a drive-in movie or cruising the streets to enjoy the neon lights. But instead, they parked in front of Casa Della Tires and told more stories about their lives before they rolled into town.

Lightning smiled as he listened to his friends tell their tales. He was glad he'd found his way to Radiator Springs. He couldn't think of a better place to call home.

Racing Days in Radiator Springs

One afternoon, the cars in Radiator Springs gathered eagerly at Flo's V8 Café. Lightning McQueen was meeting them there. He had some big news to share.

"Hey, guys," Lightning said when he rolled up, "thanks for meeting me. Doc and I wanted to tell you about our plans for the town. We want to open my racing headquarters here."

"That's right," Doc Hudson chimed in. He smiled. He was a racing legend and Lightning's new crew chief.

"There will be a real track and a large stadium to hold everyone who wants to come see a race," he explained.

Mater showed the cars a picture of what the stadium would look like.

"Hmm," said Sally, the shiny blue sports car. "This could be what puts Radiator Springs back on the map."

"That's the plan!" Lightning exclaimed.

It wasn't long before the track was ready. Lightning and Doc were excited. They decided to host a race to officially open the stadium.

They sent invitations to racers from around the world. They wanted the opening race at Radiator Springs' stadium to be a big event.

When the week of the race arrived, visitors flooded into town. The store owners in Radiator Springs were very happy to have customers again. But they weren't prepared for so many!

A line of cars waiting for new tires stretched around the block

at Casa Della Tires. Luigi and Guido had to work long after their normal closing time to help every car.

"Mamma mia!" Luigi said. "The cars, they just keep-a coming!"

The line for Flo's V8 café stretched down the street. Her customers couldn't all fit into the parking lot, so she tried bringing cans of oil to them. But she couldn't get around the traffic and ended up spilling oil on her hood.

Meanwhile, Sheriff was having a hard time keeping the race cars in line.

Otto had come all the way from Germany. He was used to driving fast everywhere he went. But Sheriff wanted him to follow the speed limit.

When Sheriff gave Otto a speeding ticket, it didn't help. Otto just thought Sheriff wanted his autograph!

That night, Sally and Sarge had to set up tents for the visiting cars because her motel didn't have any more rooms.

By the time they were finished, Sally was exhausted.

"I'm glad we have visitors again, but I didn't think there would be this much work," she told Lightning.

The race car knew his friends were tired from a long day of

taking care of so many customers. He suggested they take some time to have fun.

They decided to cruise through town. The neon lights were shining. Seeing the town lit up and full of visitors made everyone happy.

The next day, it was time for the Radiator Springs track's opening race.

Mater, Sarge, Sally, Lizzie, and Flo gathered to watch from the box seats.

Down on the track, Lightning met his competitors. He knew it would be a tough race. But he wanted to make his friends proud.

"And they're off!" Mater announced. The cars sped into their first turn.

"Lightning McQueen is in third place, but don't worry," the tow truck continued. "He'll win by the end. He's the best—"

"Mater," Sally interrupted, "you need to announce the positions of *all* the cars."

"But Lightning's my best friend," Mater said into the microphone. "And he's the best car in the race."

Down on the track, Lightning smiled. He revved his engine and soon he was even with Otto, who was in first place.

On the last turn, Lightning pulled ahead and Otto began to drop back!

Lightning stuck out his tongue as he crossed the finish line. He wanted to make sure he was the winner.

Mater cheered as he announced that his best friend had won.

"Thanks, everyone!" Lightning said to the crowd and the visiting race cars. "This was a great race, but it won't be the last here in Radiator Springs!"

The cars cheered. They couldn't wait until the next race!

Guido's
Big Surprise

Luigi was bursting with excitement. He was planning a racing-themed surprise party for his assistant and best friend, Guido. They were both big racing fans.

Guido rolled to a stop beside his friend outside Casa Della Tires.

"Today is-a going to be a good-a day, eh, Guido?" Luigi said.

The little forklift sighed. Then he turned and went into the store, ready to get to work.

Luigi chuckled. "He has-a no idea! My friend is-a in for a big-a surprise."

Just then, Ramone pulled up. "Hey, man, I'm here for my new tires," he said.

"Perfecto!" Luigi exclaimed. "Come on-a inside."

"Has Guido figured out the surprise?" Ramone whispered before they went in.

"No, it's-a still a secret," Luigi replied.

Luigi and Ramone went inside. "Guido," Luigi said, "Signore Ramone is here for his-a new tires."

Guido went into the back room to get them.

"How is your-a lovely lady, Flo?" Luigi asked Ramone.

"She's doing fine," Ramone said as Guido reappeared. "She just got a new shipment of fuel that is mighty smooth. You should stop in for a sip."

"Yes, maybe we'll-a come over later." Luigi winked at Ramone. He knew that the surprise party would take place at Flo's V8 Café. Then he noticed the tires Guido had found. Two were flat, and the other two were covered with mud.

"Guido," Luigi said slowly, "I put those-a tires in the junk pile this-a morning."

The little forklift looked at the tires he was holding and his eyes widened. He hurried back to the storeroom.

"He looks blue, man," Ramone said.

Luigi frowned. "Of course he looks-a blue. He is *always* the color blue."

Ramone laughed. "No, I meant that Guido looks sad."

When Guido returned with the correct tires, Luigi watched him. Guido did look sad. Luigi hoped the party would cheer him up.

"What's-a bugging you, Guido?" Luigi asked later.

But the only response was a loud, *"Ka-chow!"* as Lightning McQueen rolled into the store, followed by Mater.

"Hey, guys," said Lightning, "I'm here to practice for my next big race. You'll be my pit crew again. Right, Guido?"

The forklift nodded.

"Here's the plan," Lightning said. "Picture me speeding down the track. You be ready for the pit stop, okay?"

"He's-a ready," Luigi answered.

Guido got into his pit-stop position.

Vroom. "I'm heading for the pit stop," Lightning pretended, "and you're ready to change my tires in 2.5 seconds flat. And . . . go!"

Guido set to work. Luigi and Mater counted. But Guido was working very slowly.

"Two and a half-a," Luigi said, drawing out the numbers. "Three-a . . ."

"Three, four, five," Mater counted.

It took Guido five seconds—double his usual time!

"Mamma mia!" Luigi exclaimed. "Uh . . . Guido didn't sleep-a so good last night. Tomorrow, he will be back to his-a speedy self."

Lightning nodded, but he looked worried. He turned and followed Mater out of the store.

"Hey, buddy, what would our country be called if every car was painted pink?" the tow truck said. He barely paused before shouting, "A pink car*nation*!" Get it, "car" and "nation"?

Luigi turned to his friend. "What's-a wrong, Guido?" he asked. "You cannot go on being down in the Dumpster."

"Hello, boys," Sally said as she rolled in. "There's a customer at my motel who needs her tires checked. Do you have some time?"

Guido perked up a little. He went to grab his toolbox.

"Guido will take-a good care of her," Luigi said.

Sally smiled. "I knew I could count on you guys. Come on, Guido. I'll take you over to meet her." Then she turned back to Luigi and said, "I'm heading over to Flo's afterward if you need me."

"*Grazie*, Sally," Luigi replied.

After Guido left, Luigi circled the shop, cleaning things up. He saw a wrench lying on the floor and went to put it with the rest of Guido's tools. When Luigi opened the chest, he saw a postcard from Italy. It was from Guido's cousin, Guidoni.

Luigi gasped. "Guido is-a homesick! That's-a why he's so sad."

Luigi put the wrench and the card in the chest. Then he raced over to Flo's. They had to change their racing-themed surprise party to a grand Italian celebration.

Flo was serving drinks to Lightning, Sally, Mater, and Ramone at her café when Luigi appeared.

"He's-a sick!" Luigi exclaimed.

The other cars gathered around him. "Who's sick?" Sally asked.

"Guido!" Luigi cried. "He's-a homesick for his family in Italy. I thought he was-a missing the excitement of a race. But now I'm sure he's been sad because he misses his-a home."

"Well," said Sally, "Guido has a home right here in Radiator Springs—and we're going to cheer him up."

"That's right," said Flo. "We'll just change our racing party to an Italian party! I'll see if Fillmore has an olive-oil flavored brew. That would be perfecto."

Lightning smiled. "You can count on me to bring Italian racing flags for decorations."

"And Flo's got some old Italian classics on the car-aoke machine," Ramone chimed in. "'Lugnut Prima' is one of our favorites."

Luigi smiled as his friends piped up with more ideas for the party. "*Grazie*," Luigi said. "This will mean-a so much to Guido."

Luigi left Flo, Sally, and Ramone at the café to keep planning, while he went with Lightning and Mater to find Red the fire truck. They had a great idea for a big finale.

Luckily, Red agreed. He couldn't wait to be part of the surprise.

That night, Luigi could barely contain his excitement. "It's-a been a long day, eh, Guido," he said. "What do you say we go over to Flo's for a sip of oil?"

Guido gave a little nod, then followed Luigi out the door.

When they arrived at Flo's, all of the inside lights were off. It looked like the café was closed.

"I wonder what's-a going on?" Luigi said, trying to hide a smile. "Let's go in and see."

As soon as they rolled into the café, the lights came on. "*Viva Italiano*, Guido!" Flo said. The other cars all cheered.

Guido looked around in awe. There were Italian flags hanging on the walls, and lots of red, white, and green balloons filled the café.

There were posters of famous Italian landmarks. Mater stopped beside the one of the Leaning Tower of Tires. "Hey, this here picture looks a lot like the tower outside Luigi's store," he said.

Mater rolled up to the front of the café. "Can I have everyone's attention, please?"

Ramone dimmed the lights until a single spotlight shone on the tow truck.

"Now for a real surprise," he said. "Red will perform an Italian opera selection."

Red shyly moved into the spotlight. Flo started up the car-aoke machine. Beautiful music filled the air, and Red began to sing.

"*Mamma mia!*" Luigi said. "It's *bellissimo.*"

Guido closed his eyes as he listened. He felt like he was back home in Italy listening to opera with his family.

When Red finished, all the cars were speechless. The fire truck quickly moved out of the spotlight.

"Red, that was just beautiful," Sally said.

"You made this-a night so very special," Luigi said.

Red smiled shyly.

Flo set to work making sure everyone had enough oil. Mater told Red and Lightning some more jokes.

Luigi pulled his friend aside. "You are-a happy again now?" he asked Guido.

The little forklift beamed and waved an Italian flag. There was no need to be homesick when he was already right at home in Radiator Springs.

Rumble at the
Rust Bucket

It was opening day at Rust Bucket Stadium. Cars of all makes, shapes, and sizes were driving into the stands.

Mater drove into the stadium with his best friend, Lightning McQueen. "Welcome to my new stadium," said the tow truck. "Now you're not the only one with a fancy new place to play. We can do all kinds of stuff here."

"Wow, this is amazing," said Lightning as he rolled to a stop. He looked around. "I've never been in a stadium like this before!"

"That's because this is the very first stadium that I ever owned and designed," Mater replied.

The crowd began to cheer as Mater swung his tow hook in the air like a lasso.

"Welcome, cars, trucks, and vans to Rust Bucket Stadium," he hollered. "Where a truck can be a truck. Now it's time for some tire-snagging!"

Mater grabbed the first tire with his hook.

Suddenly, an engine roared. VROOM! It grew louder and louder!

"That sounds like Bubba," Mater said.

Bubba was a big orange tow truck who made a racket wherever he went. He liked to bully smaller trucks into doing anything he wanted. He smiled as he pulled into the stadium with his friends Tater and Tater Junior.

"Last time I saw him, he tried to take my hood," Mater whispered to Lightning. "But I outsmarted that big truck!"

"Mater!" exclaimed Bubba. "I think it's time for us to find out who is the best tow truck around. I challenge you to a truck derby. The winner gets to keep the Rust Bucket!"

"You're on!" Mater cried. "No tow truck is greater than Mater."

"All right, Bubba," Lightning said, "if you beat Mater, you win the Rust Bucket. But if Mater wins, you can't come back to the stadium, or to Radiator Springs. Deal?"

"Deal," said Bubba. "If I lose, I'll never set one tire in Carburetor County ever again."

"Uhh . . . Lightning," Mater said, "if I lose, can I stay in Radiator Springs? This is my home and . . ."

"Mater," Lightning said with a smile, "of course you can stay in town. But try to beat Bubba so he leaves!"

Mater and Bubba agreed to compete in three events: tire-snagging, cone-dodging, and a one-lap race around a dirt track. Whoever won the most events would be the Rust Bucket champion!

Lightning gave his friend some last-minute encouragement. "Remember, Mater, you're quicker than quick. And you're the world's best backward driver! Go and show Bubba what you're made of!"

"All right, buddy," Mater said.

The two tow trucks faced each other, hood-to-hood.

"We're going to need judges for this competition," said Bubba.

"And my pals Tater and Tater Junior will be perfect."

"We get to be judges?" said Tater Junior. "That's terrific!"

"I can't wait to tell all my friends at the garage!" Tater said.

Lightning was worried about letting Bubba's friends be the judges. But Mater was sure he could win no matter what.

"All right, boys, you've got the job," said Mater. "Go on up to the judges' stand so we can get this thing started."

Tire-snagging was the first event. Guido balanced a huge stack of tires on his lift and waited for the signal.

"Let the tire-snagging begin!" shouted Tater Junior.

Guido threw the tires into the air. Both tow trucks used their cables and hooks to snag as many tires as they could.

Mater quickly snagged four tires. But Bubba was fast, too. He hooked four as well.

Bubba didn't want Mater to win. When he saw that they were tied, he used his hook to knock a tire away from Mater.

The rest of the tires hit the ground, and the event was over. The judges took a quick count.

"Mater has three tires," said Tater Junior. "But Bubba has four. Bubba wins!"

"But he cheated!" Lightning yelled. He turned to the judges. "Didn't you see that?"

Tater shook his head. "Sorry, we must have missed it," he said.

Next up was cone-dodging. Mater and Bubba slowly pulled up to the starting line.

"You're going down," growled Bubba.

"Doubt it!" replied Mater. He looked out over the track where cones were set up for the trucks to drive around. Mater had raced around this track plenty of times.

At the signal, Mater and Bubba took off.

"*Yee-haw!*" yelled Mater as he edged ahead of Bubba. He weaved around the cones with ease.

The big truck couldn't stay on the track. Bubba kept sliding when he tried to turn in the dust.

The dust didn't bother Mater, though. When he slid, he just turned around and drove backward. He moved between the cones and didn't hit a single one!

The crowd went wild when Mater crossed the finish line first. Bubba was still on the track, coughing up dust and surrounded by cones.

"Mater wins!" said Tater Junior.

CARS STORYBOOK COLLECTION

Mater and Bubba rolled up to the starting line for the last race. Bubba wasn't happy. He didn't like to lose.

"You won that one, but you'll never beat me in an all-out race!" said Bubba as he revved his engine.

"May the best truck win," said Mater.

"I will!" Bubba yelled.

The race started, and the trucks took off. Bubba used his powerful engine to pull ahead of Mater. Then he dropped his hook and cable to the ground and let it drag behind him. He really wanted to win this event.

"Watch out, Mater!" yelled Lightning.

Mater dodged the sharp hook swinging across the road in front of him.

Suddenly, Bubba's hook got caught on a rock! Bubba was jerked back into the air, where he flipped and landed on his side.

"*Oww!* Help me!" he cried.

Mater slammed on his brakes.

"Hold on, Bubba! I'll get you back on your tires in a jiffy," he said.

Mater swung his tow cable toward Bubba and latched it onto his roof. He pulled and pulled with all his might. But the big truck was too heavy for him to flip over. Then Mater had an idea.

"Tater! Tater Junior! Get over here!" yelled Mater. "I need your help lifting Bubba!"

The three tow trucks used their hooks to pull Bubba off his side and set him back on all four tires.

"Nice teamwork!" said Lightning as the crowd cheered. Tater and Tater Junior smiled.

"Thanks," muttered Bubba. Then he quickly drove out of the stadium, embarrassed.

"Well, I guess that makes you the winner," said Tater Junior.

The crowd cheered for Mater—the Rust Bucket champion!

"Uh, Mr. Tow Mater," said Tater, "can you teach us a few of your tricks?"

"Sure!" replied Mater.

Guido tossed some tires into the air. Mater coached the tow trucks until they got it. They soon found out it was harder than it looked!

Double Trouble

Lightning McQueen was a talented race car. But he knew he had to practice if he wanted to keep winning.

He spent a lot of time working on his speed and trying new tricks. Doc Hudson coached him.

"Remember to hold steady on that turn," said Doc as they cruised around a bend.

"Got it," said Lightning.

Behind them, Mater was practicing his best skill— driving backward.

"Better watch out! I'm right on your tail!" he called to his friend.

"Not for long!" Lightning shouted. He hit the gas and zoomed down the track.

"What a pair," Doc said with a laugh.

Chick Hicks was Lightning's biggest rival. He was a sneaky race car with lots of dirty tricks. Instead of practicing, Chick just studied new ways to cheat.

When Chick heard about all the time Lightning was putting in, he challenged him to a race. He wanted to beat Lightning on his own track.

Chick decided that he and Lightning should each race with a partner. Lightning chose Mater, and Chick chose a young race car named Switcher.

"Those two don't have a chance," Chick said with a laugh.

Switcher was a sleek gray car with a mean streak just like Chick's. Both cars were willing to do anything to win—even cheat. Because of that, they would be a tough team to beat.

Chick wanted to make sure Switcher was in top shape. The young car was fast, but he didn't have much racing experience. Chick trained him for hours every day, teaching him how to race and how to cheat his opponents.

"You call that speed?" Chick yelled. He stood on a podium at the side of the track as Switcher came around a bend. "My grandma Hicks can drive faster than you!"

Switcher narrowed his eyes. He didn't like being called slow. He revved his engine. *Vroom!* Soon, he was driving faster than Chick had ever seen him go.

Chick grinned. "That's more like it!" he said. "I can't wait to beat Lightning on his fancy new track in front of all his fans."

On the day of the race, Radiator Springs Speedway was filled with the sounds of honking horns and screaming spectators. Fans had come from miles around to watch Lightning and Mater race Chick and Switcher. The stands were packed—bumper to bumper.

The crowd roared when the four cars rolled up to the starting line.

Mater smiled at Lightning. He knew they could beat Chick and Switcher.

But Switcher was just as confident that his team would win. He looked over at Lightning and Mater. "That's our competition?" he said loudly to Chick. "I could beat them with my eyes closed."

"You should both keep your eyes closed while you're driving in our dust," Lightning said. *"Ka-chow!"*

The cars revved their engines, and the crowd went wild.

Suddenly, the green flag waved. All four cars took off around the track.

Lightning took the lead right away. But Chick and Switcher were able to catch up after the first turn. Lightning could feel Chick gaining on him.

Bam! Chick rammed Lightning's bumper. "Watch out, rookie," said Chick. "I wouldn't want you to get hurt out here."

From his spot in the rear, Mater saw Chick's dirty trick. "Hey, that's not racing, that's cheating!" the tow truck called out.

But Lightning was used to Chick's nasty moves. And he had a surprise for his rival.

"I'd better get out of your way, Chick," said Lightning. He fired up his brand-new turbo speeder and drove off. "See you at the finish line!" he called. He left Chick in the dust.

Mater gave a whoop of delight. "That's my partner!"

Chick snarled as he watched Lightning shoot ahead. He pulled up next to Switcher. "Go get him," he said.

Switcher grinned. He had a turbo speeder of his own. He fired it up and caught Lightning in just a few seconds.

"What took you so long?" Lightning asked with a laugh.

Switcher didn't respond. Instead, he pulled ahead of Lightning and released a stream of oil.

Lightning tried to swerve, but he drove right into the oil and began to skid. He spun in a circle.

Switcher raced past him, laughing.

Chick caught up to Switcher on the next turn.

"He didn't even know what hit him," Switcher said. "No one can beat me!" He hit the gas and sped ahead of Chick.

Chick grew angry. He didn't care that Switcher was his partner. He wanted to cross the finish line first!

"That tin can better not think he's beating me," said Chick. He revved his engine and took off after Switcher.

Suddenly—BAM! Chick rammed right into Switcher. "It's time you learned a lesson," he growled. "No one beats Chick Hicks."

Switcher lost control and went skidding across the track. He hit a patch of dirt and flipped over—twice! Finally, he came to a stop in the infield. His front bumper was crushed and his tires were twisted. He couldn't believe what Chick had done.

"I'm on your team!" cried Switcher.

"Not anymore!" shouted Chick as he sped past his teammate.

Lightning was back on the track, and Mater was close behind him. They were shocked by what Chick had done. They'd known he was a cheater, but they hadn't thought he would crash into his own racing partner. Now Lightning was even more determined to beat Chick.

Vroom! Lightning put on a burst of speed. He started to gain on Chick.

After a few minutes, Lightning needed a pit stop. He and Mater both pulled over to the sidelines where Doc and their crew were waiting.

"Tires!" yelled Luigi.

Guido zipped over and changed Lightning's and Mater's tires. Then he and Sarge filled up both cars with gas.

"I can't believe Chick did that to his own teammate," Lightning said to Doc. "I think it's time to give him a taste of his own fuel."

"No," said Doc. "I think it's time to put our own plan into action. Listen carefully and follow my instructions."

With fresh tires and full tanks of gas, Lightning and Mater burst back onto the track. There were only a few laps to go!

Doc gave Lightning and Mater directions over the radio. First, he told Mater to get in front of Chick and start swerving back and forth.

Mater pulled ahead. Every time Chick tried to pass him, the tow truck spun backward and blocked his path.

"Stop it, you hunk of junk!" Chick yelled.

"Driving backward is my specialty," teased Mater. "I can give you lessons if you want."

While Chick was distracted, Doc told Lightning to move ahead on the inside track. The race car hit the gas.

Before Chick knew what had happened, Lightning raced across the finish line. Mater followed right behind him.

"Noooo!" cried Chick.

Lightning and Mater whooped with delight.

Lightning, Mater, and Doc drove onto the winner's stand. They were presented with a shiny silver trophy.

Chick glared at them. "I'll get you next time, Lightning," he said.

"I can't wait to see you try," Lightning said. He and Mater posed with their trophy as reporters snapped pictures.

"Great teamwork today, you two," said Doc.

The two friends smiled. They had worked together and won— no cheating necessary.

All's Well at the
Wheel Well

CARS STORYBOOK COLLECTION

Radiator Springs was bustling with activity. The grand reopening of the Wheel Well Motel was in less than a week.

Sally the shiny blue sports car was very excited. Ever since the famous race car Lightning McQueen had moved his racing headquarters to Radiator Springs, the town had been filled with visitors. When all the rooms at the Cozy Cone Motel had been booked for weeks and weeks, Sally decided it was time to reopen the Wheel Well.

"Radiator Springs is back on the map," she had told her friends. "Now, we need another motel for all the cars that visit."

The townsfolk had agreed with Sally. They were happy to see visitors return to the town. And they were eager to help Sally fix up the old motel.

"We'll be the most popular place in Carburetor County!" Sally cheered.

Ramone helped Sally decorate the rooms inside the motel. He gave each one its own style. "Then cars will want to return to check out the different looks," the hot rod explained.

Sally's favorite was a room overlooking the valley. Ramone had painted a mural of Radiator Springs at night showing the stores with their neon lights.

"This is great, Ramone!" Sally exclaimed. "My two favorite views are in one room."

While Ramone fixed up the inside of the motel, Red helped Sally spruce up the outside.

The fire engine had created new flower displays for the motel. He watered each patch once a day and drove out to the motel at least twice more to make sure everything looked perfect for the grand reopening.

When Lightning McQueen rolled back into town, he found Mater, Flo, and Sheriff at Flo's V8 Café.

"Welcome back, buddy," the tow truck said with a wide smile. "We sure missed you around here."

"Thanks, Mater. I'm glad to be home," Lightning said. The race car had been traveling to different events in the past few weeks. But no matter how many trophies he won, he was always eager to get back to Radiator Springs. "I love racing, but it's nice to slow down every now and then."

"Well, you don't have much time before things speed up here," Flo told him. "Sally's opening the new Wheel Well in just three days."

"Really? Is she ready? Maybe I should go out there and see if she needs any help," Lightning said.

"I'll race you!" Mater exclaimed. "Last one there has to clean my wheel wells!"

A few minutes later, Lightning skidded to a stop in front of the Wheel Well. He was just ahead of Mater.

"Aw, shucks," Mater said. "I almost had you."

"Next time I'll race you driving backwards. You'll win for sure," Lightning replied. He looked up at the motel. "Wow, Sally really has fixed this place up."

"Everybody helped," Mater said. "I got to tow old shrubs out of the way so Red could plant the new flowers. And I promised Miss Sally I would give all her customers free backward driving lessons!"

The two cars rolled over to Guido and Luigi. They'd brought some tires out from Luigi's store, Casa Della Tires. Guido was creating a new tire display for the reopening.

"You are just in-a time," Luigi said, when he saw the race car and tow truck. "Guido is almost-a finished."

Guido put the last tire into place. Then he rolled back to admire his work.

"It's a wheel . . . made of wheels," Lightning said slowly.

"That's-a right!" Luigi crowed proudly.

"Hey, Stickers," Sally said as she drove over. "When did you get back to town?"

"Just a little while ago," Lightning replied. "This place looks great, Sally. Is there anything I can do to help you get ready?"

"You've already done more than enough," Sally said. "You brought customers back to our town by setting up your racing headquarters here." She smiled and went to check on one of the rooms.

"Miss Sally sure does like you," Mater said to his friend. *"Whoo-eee!"*

"Oh, come on, Mater. Sally's just excited about reopening the motel. I wish I could think of something to do to make the day even more special for her," Lightning said. "I'm gonna go for a drive. Maybe that will help me think."

"Okay, buddy," Mater said. "Just remember to keep your wheels on the road!"

Lightning drove down the mountain and through the valley. He passed the old dirt track he used to practice on. He slowed down as he rolled into the center of town.

The cars that weren't helping out at the Wheel Well were getting their stores ready for the extra customers who would come for the reopening. Lightning saw Lizzie out in front of her store, Radiator Springs Curios. He rolled over to say hello.

"Stanley would have gotten all steamed up if he could see the town today," Lizzie said. "Why, the Wheel Well was one of his favorite spots!"

Lizzie slapped a sticker on Lightning's front bumper and went back to tidying up her shop.

Lightning looked at the bumper sticker in a reflection on an old hubcap. It read: ALL'S WELL AT THE WHEEL WELL. He smiled. Lizzie always had the perfect sticker.

Lightning left Lizzie, but he couldn't stop thinking of what she'd said about Stanley, who had founded the town. If only he could see Radiator Springs today!

Then he thought about what Sally had said—that he'd been the one to bring visitors back to town.

"All because of a little racing," he murmured. Suddenly, he had an idea!

A race car couldn't paint rooms at the motel or sell stickers. But he could help Sally make headlines at the opening with a trick or two. He zoomed off to tell Sally his idea—and to start practicing.

For the next two days, Lightning worked on his trick.
Mater drove out to the old track and watched him take turn
after turn. "You're up to something!" he called out to his friend.
Lightning only smiled and kept practicing.

The morning of the grand reopening, the cars from Radiator Springs were gathered in front of the Wheel Well with press cars and visitors. Everyone was excited. The cars oohed and aahed over the motel.

"Ladies and gentlecars," Sally greeted everyone. "It is my pleasure to welcome you to the historic Wheel Well Motel, once again open to all the travelers who come to Radiator Springs. And now, to kick off the festivities, Lightning McQueen would like to give you an official Wheel Well welcome!"

There was a loud *vroom*. Lightning zipped around the press cars. When he was right in front of Sally, he turned and lifted his two left wheels at the same time to wave to the crowd.

The press cars snapped photos, and the crowd cheered loudly.

Then Lightning looped around Sally and waved with his two right wheels.

The crowd went wild.

A few minutes later, Sally invited everyone inside for a tour. She stood by the door and welcomed each car.

When Lightning pulled up beside her, she smiled. "You really got the crowd excited about the motel. You care about this town a lot."

Lightning beamed. "Getting lost here was the best thing that ever happened to me," he said. "It's my home."

Sally looked at the bumper sticker on Lightning's front fender. "Nice sticker," she said as she rolled inside.

Lightning laughed as he followed her. All *was* well at the Wheel Well . . . and in Radiator Springs.

Deputy Mater

Early one morning, Sally the shiny blue sports car was busy working at the Cozy Cone Motel. She'd had a lot of customers lately. Radiator Springs was full of visiting cars hoping to catch a glimpse of Lightning McQueen!

Sally heard a loud *vroom* outside. "Lightning must be back from his latest race," she said to herself. She rolled outside to welcome him home.

But Lightning wasn't the one revving his engine. Three tricked-out cars with loud engines—and even louder radios— zoomed through town.

Sally didn't like to see other cars ruining the peace and quiet. She drove over to Flo's V8 Café to see if anyone else had seen—or heard—the fancy cars zipping through town.

She found Sheriff and Fillmore at the café. Sheriff was trying to explain why the traffic light only flashed yellow.

"That tells cars to drive carefully," Sheriff said. "They should slow down, but they don't have to stop if there's no other traffic."

"Good morning," Sally said. "Did you see those cars that just raced through town? They could use a lesson in traffic laws!"

"I've seen those cars around before," Sheriff said. "I haven't been able to catch them yet. They don't follow the speed limit, and I bet they don't even know we have a traffic light in town."

Sally and Sheriff drove down Main Street. They wanted to see if any other cars had seen the speeders.

"Oh, no!" Sally said when they saw Red, the shy fire engine. He was looking at his garden. The speeding cars had run over the flowers! "Those cars have ruined Red's garden!"

"I know, Sally," Sheriff said with a sigh. "But I can't be everywhere in town at one time."

Sally agreed. Tracking down cars who wouldn't follow the town's driving rules was a big job. With all the tourists coming through, Sheriff had been busier than ever!

"What if we helped?" Sally said. "You could name some cars as deputies. They could watch over certain places in town when you can't be there."

"That's a great idea!" Fillmore said. "I bet lots of cars would be willing to help."

"Howdy, folks," Mater called out as he drove toward them. "What's rolling down Main Street? Besides me!"

The tow truck laughed loudly.

"Mater, why are your sides white?" Sally asked.

"Oh, shoot," Mater said. "I asked Ramone if he could patch up my rusty spots and he had the wrong paint in the sprayer."

"Looks like the perfect spot for a sticker," Fillmore said.

"Or . . . a deputy badge!" Sally said. "Mater, would you want to help Sheriff catch any rule-breakers who come through town?"

"Me?" Mater asked. "Why sure, Miss Sally. I've always wanted to stop ruler-breaking. I—"

"No, Mater," Sheriff interrupted. "As a deputy, you'll be on the lookout for rule-breaker cars who can't follow the speed limit or obey the laws of our town."

Mater was eager to start helping Sheriff!

Sally rounded up all the cars in town. They gathered at the courthouse, where Sheriff made Mater an honorary deputy.

Then, Mater was allowed to choose some other cars to help him. He picked Sally, Sarge, and Lightning McQueen.

They were made honorary deputies, too.

After all of Mater's deputies were sworn in, Ramone painted a Radiator Springs badge on their doors. Then the cars set to work.

Mater assigned each deputy an area to watch over. Lightning kept an eye on the intersection with the blinking yellow light. He was right across the street from Flo's. She had extra cans of oil at the ready for all the new deputies.

Sarge took up a position near Lightning. He used his long-range binoculars to look for cars approaching the town.

Sally drove around to all the stores. She chatted with the owners to make sure they were happy with their customers.

The town was quiet and peaceful—just the way the cars wanted it!

Mater drove through town, keeping an eye out for rule-breaking cars. He also checked in with each of his deputies.

"This is a tough job," he told Lightning. "But I'm just the tow truck to do it!"

Lightning smiled. His friend was doing a great job. There hadn't been any sign of trouble in town for the whole day!

Suddenly, they heard Sarge call out, "Incoming! Speeding cars approaching town!"

All the deputies gathered on Main Street. Mater rolled to the front of the crowd.

The cars could feel the thump of loud music through their tires. They waited for the visitors to come into view.

"They're the same cars that sped through here the other day," Sally whispered to Lightning.

"We'll stop them this time, Sally," Lightning assured her. "Deputy Mater's ready to tell those cars who's in charge."

The tricked-out cars rolled to a stop in front of Mater.

"Howdy, out-of-towners," Mater greeted them. "We're glad to have you visit. But we've had some complaints that you aren't following our rules."

The car with the radio turned down his music. "What rules?" he asked.

"Well, see, we have a speed limit here," Mater said. "And your radio is so loud I can't hear my own engine clunking."

"Isn't that the speed limit?" one of the cars asked. He pointed toward the "66" posted at the side of the road.

Mater looked at the sign. He chuckled. Then he burst out laughing. "That does look like a speed-limit sign," he said. "But it's really the route number of the road you're driving on. And this little town is the nicest stop you'll find in all of Carburetor County."

"Anyhow," Mater continued, "this little light is more important than the speed limit."

Mater swung his tow hook up to the blinking yellow traffic light.

"Sheriff told me that this means slow down," Mater said. "So whenever you see a yellow light, hit the brakes before you break the rules."

"That sounds easy enough," one of the cars said. The others agreed.

Mater invited the out-of-towners to stay for a can of oil at Flo's. The cars followed Mater slowly down the street to the café.

All the deputies joined them. They'd had fun helping Sheriff keep order in town. And now they were ready to celebrate a job well done!

Lightning
in Paradise

Lightning McQueen was used to life in the fast lane. After traveling to different cities for race after race, he knew how to handle the press and the fans. And his driving skills were better than ever. He also knew how to have fun!

"I could get used to this!" Lightning told Sally. They had just arrived in Santa Carburera for Lightning's latest event. His biggest rival, Chick Hicks, had challenged him to a race in paradise.

Sally looked around at the swaying palm trees, the sandy beaches, and all the tour cars crowding the pier. "Me, too," she said.

"Let's go check out some of the hot spots," Lightning said. "We can relax for a while."

"Don't you want to check out the course before Chick shows up?" Sally asked. She wanted Lightning to keep his focus. There would be plenty of time to take in the sights after he won the race.

Lightning flashed his brightest smile. "C'mon, Sally," he said. "I know Chick's moves. I could outrace him in my sleep! Let's go have some fun."

Sally was about to give in. She was eager to go for a drive. But just then, she saw Chick Hicks coming down the road. A shiny pink car drove beside him.

"Hey, Lightning," Sally said slowly. "Are you sure you're racing Chick? Not one of his students?"

The last few times Lightning thought he would be facing off with Chick, at the last minute Chick had brought in a new opponent. He had been training rookie race cars when he wasn't racing himself. They were all fast. But worst of all, Chick had taught them to cheat.

Chick and the pink car pulled to a stop beside Lightning and Sally. "Hey, there, Lightning," Chick said, "have you met Candice? She's the hottest new car on the track since . . . well, since you!" He laughed.

Before Lightning could respond, press cars and fans flooded the pier. Their cameras flashed, and they asked for Candice's autograph.

Candice smiled. She loved all the attention.

Lightning was speechless. He had never heard of Candice!
But the fans and press certainly had. They didn't even notice that
Lightning was there.

"That's what happens, I guess," Chick said. "You hide in a
small town, and everyone forgets about you. Real winners stay in
the fast lane."

Sally was furious. She pulled Lightning away from the crowd
on the pier.

"What a show-off!" Sally cried. She and Lightning coasted down a quiet road. "I can't believe her. Or Chick!"

Lightning chuckled. "It's okay, Sally," he said. "Don't let her get to you. Besides, we have better things to do than pose for the cameras."

"Like get ready for the race?" Sally asked.

"Exactly," Lightning said with a smile. "I'm going to go practice my turns in the sand. Then we'll go sightseeing, all right?"

"Of course! You're going to show Chick and Candice that working hard in a small town is better than ten minutes of fame in the fast lane," Sally said.

Lightning practiced for the rest of the afternoon. By the time he had finished, he was beat. He decided to go to bed early to rest up for the race.

Sally went for a drive. The night was cool, and the full moon lit up the road with a blue glow.

Suddenly, Sally heard loud music coming from a nearby tent. She drove over to take a look.

Inside, she saw Chick and Candice. They were surrounded by fans. Everyone was sipping oil and having a good time.

"Lightning was right," Sally said to herself as she drove away. "Candice is only here to have fun. She's not ready for a real race. Lightning will have no trouble winning tomorrow!"

The next morning, Lightning pulled up to the starting line.

"Lightning," Candice said sweetly, "would you mind moving back a little? You're blocking my good side." She smiled, and the cameras flashed.

Lightning couldn't believe it. The race was about to begin, and Candice was still posing for pictures!

"Focus," Lightning told himself. "I am speed. I am Lightning."

But it was hard to stay focused. The cameras flashed in his eyes. The fans chanted from the side of the road. "Candice! Candice! Candice!"

Lightning closed his eyes. "Come on, focus!" he said. But he couldn't drown out all the noise.

Suddenly, the announcer's voice came over the loudspeaker. "Race cars to the starting line. The race will begin in one minute."

"Go get 'em, Candice!" Chick Hicks called out.

"Cars, take your mark," the announcer said.

Lightning and Candice sped off. Lightning quickly took the lead!

But Candice didn't let him get too far ahead. On the first turn, She pulled even with him, and then coasted in ahead. She put on a burst of speed.

When Lightning tried to pass her on the outside, she tilted her body toward the sun. The light bounced off her shiny pink paint, right into Lightning's eyes!

"*Ahh!*" Lightning cried. He blinked furiously, but it was no use. With the light blinding him, he couldn't see where he was going. He drove off the track and into a patch of sand.

Candice drove off laughing.

Lightning shook the sand out of his eyes. He pulled back onto the track. He was angry—at Candice and at himself. He knew Chick liked to cheat. He should have known Candice would, too.

"That's why she didn't spend any time practicing," he said to himself.

"Lightning," Sally called from the sidelines. "Hang back a little. Let Candice think she's won, then pull up fast. You'll beat her crossing the finish line."

Lightning put Sally's plan into action. He kept enough distance between himself and Candice to make her think he was out of the race.

On the next turn, Lightning started to pull even with her.

Chick Hicks was nervous as he watched from the sidelines. "Losers don't make the front page, Candice!" he called out.

Candice moved to the side of the road. As her wheels hit a patch of sand, she spun around. The sand sprayed up at Lightning. He veered off the road.

"I hate getting sand in my tires," Candice said. "But that was totally worth it!" She pulled into the lead once again.

The finish line was just ahead!

Candice smiled as she approached the finish line. She was sure her tricks had helped her beat Lightning McQueen!

"Hey, Candice," a photographer called, "how about giving us a winning smile?"

Candice turned. Suddenly, dozens of cameras flashed at once. Candice slammed on her brakes. She couldn't see with all the blinding lights!

She felt a whoosh of air. She blinked and tried not to catch a glimpse of what had just passed her.

"And Lightning McQueen wins the race!" the announcer said.

"Nooo!" Candice cried. She hadn't won after all!

Lightning made his way to the winner's circle. Sally parked beside him as he accepted his trophy.

"*Ka-chow!*" Lightning said. He smiled for the cameras. The press cars and the fans went wild!

Then, Lightning and Sally left the big crowds behind. They were ready to go for a quiet drive.

"Will you be ready to go home tomorrow?" Sally asked. "Or will you be sad to leave paradise?"

"Home *is* paradise," Lightning replied. "But I sure am glad we had this little vacation."

Then the two cars sped off into the sunset.

Ramone's Blue Idea

One day, Ramone was working in his paint shop, loading a new paint color into the sprayer when Lightning McQueen and Mater pulled up.

"Hey, Ramone, is it time for a new paint job?" Lightning asked.

"Of course!" the hot rod exclaimed. "It's my lady Flo's birthday. So I'm painting myself her favorite color: blue. And I'll stay blue for a whole week!"

"No way!" shouted Mater. "I've never seen you stay one color for that long."

"Me, either," Lightning agreed.

Ramone laughed. "I've never tried it before. But this is for my lady's big day. I want her to be happy."

Lightning and Mater nodded. They understood why Ramone wanted to stay blue. But they wondered if he could do it for seven days.

That night, all the cars in Radiator Springs gathered on Main Street. They were going to cruise under the neon lights to celebrate Flo's birthday.

"Happy birthday, Flo!" Sally said.

"Thanks, sugar," Flo replied. But she looked worried. "Have you seen Ramone?" she asked.

Suddenly, the cars heard an engine revving. The door of Ramone's House of Body Art opened. A blue Ramone rolled out. He drove over to his wife. The cars admired his new look.

"Ramone, you painted yourself blue!" Flo exclaimed. "That's my favorite color!"

"That's why I did it!" he said. "And I'll be blue all week."

"A whole week?" Flo gasped. "But you change your colors almost every day."

"Not this time," Ramone replied. "It's my gift to you. Happy birthday, Flo. Let's cruise."

Luigis
IRES
EAT
WIMPYSWIPERS
LUGS
MISS PISTON
TIPI
LUBE-O-RAMA
Rust-eze

The next day, Ramone was up early. He cleaned his shop, but it only took him a couple of hours. And he didn't have any customers waiting.

"Hmm," he said. "I could try painting myself yellow and green."

Ramone had just loaded yellow paint into his sprayer when he remembered: he had promised to stay blue for a whole week!

He decided to drive over to Flo's V8 Café. Maybe she had some customers looking for a fresh paint job.

When Ramone pulled up to the café, he saw Flo serving cans of oil to Fillmore, Sarge, and Mater.

"Hi, sugar," Flo said. "You taking a break for a sip of oil?"

"No," Ramone said. "I came to see if you wanted a new paint job. Or if you have any customers in need of a new look?"

But Flo was too busy. So were the other cars.

Ramone sighed and rolled back to his shop. He'd never had a whole day with no cars to paint before. He'd always been able to paint himself when it got slow!

For the next two days, Ramone asked all the cars in Radiator Springs if they needed new paint jobs. Not a single car did though.

Ramone rolled slowly across his shop. Then he rolled back. He didn't know what to do with himself.

Flo pulled in. "Why are you so blue?" she asked.

Ramone tried to smile, but he couldn't. He looked longingly at his paint supplies. "I wanted to be blue for you," he said.

"Honey, blue is my favorite color," Flo said. "But if you're not happy being blue, then paint yourself another color! You're my hot rod. I'd rather see you happy."

"Flo's right," Ramone heard Sally's voice call out. "We miss the old Ramone!"

The hot rod turned to see his friends parked outside the shop. They were waiting for him to try a new color!

Ramone didn't waste any time. He pulled out his paint supplies and set to work. After three days of being blue, he was ready to try every color he had!

When he was finished, he went for a drive down Main Street.

"There's my hot rod!" Flo called out.

"It's good to see the old Ramone back in town," Lightning said. "Great new colors!"

And Ramone had to agree.

Sarge's New Recruit

"**A**ttention, soldier!" Sarge called out. "You need to pick up the pace!"

Guido looked back at the jeep. He was going as fast as his little wheels could carry him. But Sarge continued to shout orders at the forklift.

Sheriff pulled up beside Sarge. "You better have a good reason for telling cars to speed through town," he said.

"Of course I do," Sarge replied. "I've started a training camp for cars who think they're tough. Luigi and Guido wanted to be my first recruits."

Sheriff and Sarge watched Guido and Luigi zip up and down Main Street. Guido would pull ahead and block Luigi's path. Then Luigi would make a quick turn and Guido had to catch up.

"What exactly are you training them to do?" Sheriff asked.

"I'm training them to be tough," Sarge said. "The cars who come to my camp will find out what they're made of."

Just then, the cars heard a loud VROOM. A big, green 4x4 rolled down Main Street.

"Sarge, it looks like you've got a new recruit," Sheriff said.

The 4x4 stopped in front of Sarge. "Hi," he said. "My name is T. J." He smiled at the cars.

"Welcome to Radiator Springs, T. J.," Sarge said. "You're just in time to join my new training camp."

"Oh, that's nice," said T. J. "But I'm not here for any training."

"You misunderstood me, soldier," Sarge said. He pulled up so close to T. J. that he could see his reflection in T. J.'s shiny door. "That wasn't an invitation. That was an order!"

Sarge rolled back over to Luigi and Guido. They lined up behind him. Sarge looked back at T. J. The 4x4 slowly rolled into line.

Sarge led the group to a rocky area just outside of town.

"Oh, no," T. J. said as he looked at the rough road. "I might get a flat tire driving here."

"No complaining," Sarge said. "You're a 4x4. You're meant to go off-road. Now, come on!"

Luigi drove beside T. J. as Sarge pulled ahead. "Don't-a worry," Luigi whispered to the 4x4. "Guido is-a much smaller than you, and he is just-a fine. Besides, if anything happens, he can-a help!"

"Pit stop!" Guido said with a smile. He could change tires faster than anyone.

The cars all made it over the bumpy road without any trouble. T. J. was surprised. He'd never driven on such rough terrain, but he was glad to know that he could.

Next, Sarge told the cars to cross a riverbed.

"It's so cold!" T. J. said as he dipped his tire into the water.

"Look at Guido," Luigi said. "If-a you move-a fast like him, you don't even notice the cold."

T. J. nodded. Then he drove through the river as fast as he could. His large wheels splashed water in every direction.

"Okay, team," Sarge said. "It's time for the final drill. We're going down that slope and across the mud puddle."

T. J. gasped. The hill was very steep. And the mud looked like it would stick to his rims for a long time.

But Sarge wouldn't let the 4x4 quit now. "You've come this far, soldier," he said. "You just need a little more courage to make it to the end."

189

T. J. started down the hill with Guido and Luigi. "Ooh," he cried, "I'm going to flip over!"

He picked up speed as he went down the hill.

"Hit the brakes!" Sarge called out.

T. J. slammed on his brakes. He skidded to the bottom and splashed into the mud.

The 4x4 began to laugh. Sarge rolled up beside him. "What's so funny?" he asked.

"I'm dirty, I'm tired, and I need a new paint job to fix all these scratches," T. J. said. "But I did it!"

"Good job, soldier," Sarge said. He smiled. He was proud of all three of his recruits. But most of all, he was happy that T. J. had stuck with it.

"Now, time to hit the car wash," Sarge said as they drove up onto the dirt road. "Tomorrow will be another full day of training."

"Sir! Yes, sir!" T. J. shouted happily.

He offered Guido and Luigi a ride on his roof rack. All the way back to town, they talked about what Sarge would have them do the next day. Would it be a relay race? Or maybe a tractor pull?

T. J. couldn't wait. He loved being at Sarge's training camp.

Tag Team

"Wow!" Lightning McQueen exclaimed as he looked around the city of Motoropolis. "This place is awesome!"

"It's real flashy," agreed Ramone. "I'm glad I freshened up my paint before we came."

Lightning's biggest rival, Chick Hicks, had challenged him to a relay race through the city at night. Lightning had invited Ramone to be his racing partner and the two had set off for Motoropolis the next day.

When they got there, Ramone was so excited that he gave Lightning a special glow-in-the-dark paint job. "This is great!" he said. "Chick Hicks will see me glowing as I speed across the finish line ahead of him!"

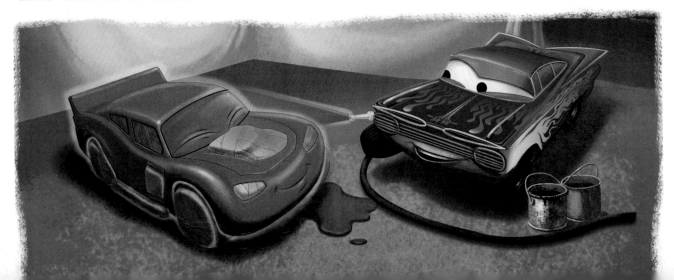

Chick Hicks and his partner, Stinger, were getting ready for the race, too. They had one plan: to win. And they were going to cheat to do it.

"Just don't let the judges catch you," Chick warned.

Stinger rammed into a stack of tires. He smiled as they went spinning in every direction.

"You're going to ram Lightning right out of this race!" Chick cried.

On the night of the race, both teams were ready. The stadium was filled with cheering cars.

The announcer introduced the relay teams. Then he reminded the cars of the rules. Ramone and Chick would begin the race and then tag their teammates at Breakaway Tunnel. Lightning and Stinger would race to the finish line.

"Good luck, Ramone," Lightning said. "I'll see you at Breakaway Tunnel!"

Ramone smiled. "I'm used to driving low and slow. But with all these fans cheering, I'm ready to hit the gas!"

Ramone and Chick rolled up to the starting line.

"I can't believe that rookie chose a hot rod to be his partner," Chick said. He revved his engine.

"I can't believe you keep asking him to race," Ramone replied. "You haven't beat him yet!"

An official waved the starting flag. The cars took off.

Ramone kept even with Chick through the first turn. Then, bit by bit, he started to pull ahead!

Suddenly, the hot rod felt Chick Hicks getting closer. The race car had blocked the outside lane and was trying to push Ramone into a brick wall! Ramone had to do something fast.

He dipped low on his wheels, then sprang up into the air. He soared over Chick's roof and landed safely in front of him.

Chick crashed into the brick wall, and sparks flew everywhere.

"Maybe that's why Lightning picked me to be his partner," Ramone said with a laugh. He zoomed away.

Ramone was in the lead, and Chick was nowhere in sight. Stinger dumped a pile of bolts into the middle of the road to stop the hot rod.

"This-s-s r-r-road is b-bumpy," Ramone said as he drove over the bolts. He was happy that Luigi and Guido had given him a new set of tough tires before the race.

Chick wasn't so lucky. *Pop! Pop! Pop!* His tires were damaged.

"Stinger!" he yelled. "Do whatever it takes to slow him down. I've got to make a pit stop."

Stinger had one more trick to try. He set up a fake roadblock
right in Ramone's path.

The hot rod slowed to a stop when he saw the signs. He wasn't
sure he should follow them, but he didn't know where else to go.
He had to get to Lightning as fast as he could!

He decided to follow the signs, which pointed him down a
one-way street.

Ramone took turn after turn. The streets were like a maze.

"Oh, man," he said, "I knew those signs looked funny. I was so close to beating Chick to Breakaway Tunnel."

Suddenly, Ramone heard shouts and cheers. Then he heard loud, roaring engines. He turned another corner and saw Breakaway Tunnel!

Lightning and Stinger were lined up, waiting to be tagged by their partners.

Ramone took off up the street. He was going so fast he almost couldn't hear the cars on the side of the road cheering him on.

"Come on, Ramone!" Lightning yelled.

As he sped toward the entrance to the tunnel, Ramone could see Chick quickly approaching. He revved his engine and raced toward Lightning.

Chick put on a burst of speed. He didn't want Ramone to tag Lightning before he could get to Stinger.

Ramone was only a few feet from Lightning when Chick caught him. He tried to push Ramone into another wall. But Ramone was ready for the trick this time.

The hot rod zoomed up the building's loading ramp and raced to the relay point. He tagged Lightning right before Chick tagged Stinger. "You're it!" he called.

Lightning took off into the tunnel.

Lightning was speeding through the tunnel when everything went dark. "Hey!" Lightning cried. Chick had turned out the tunnel lights.

Then Lightning's eyes had to adjust to a bright blue glow. "Whoa!" he said. "What's going on?"

His paint was glowing in the dark, and he could see!

"Thank you, Ramone!" Lightning said as he sped through the tunnel.

Stinger had caught up to Lightning as they exited the tunnel. "You're not so fast after all," Stinger said with a sneer. He pulled up behind Lightning and rammed his bumper.

Lightning skidded into a pothole. He couldn't move!

"Lucky hit," he said to Stinger. "I bet you couldn't do it again, though."

Stinger rolled to a stop. He looked at Lightning. Then he made a wide turn and came at him again. *BAM!*

Lightning flew out of the pothole. "Thanks!" he called out as he took off.

Stinger glared at Lightning's taillights. Then he chased after the race car.

Stinger tried to catch up to Lightning. The race was almost done! He spun his wheels as fast as he could. But Stinger was better at ramming than at racing. He was falling further behind.

"Do something!" Chick called from the sidelines. "You have to cross the finish line first!"

Stinger spotted a parking lot near the track. The finish line was just on the other side of it!

He made a sharp turn into the lot. He didn't see the DO NOT ENTER sign.

Pop! Pop! Pop! Pop!

The parking lot was full of sharp objects! All four of Stinger's tires blew.

He heard the crowd go wild as Lightning raced across the finish line in first place.

Ramone met Lightning at the winner's stand. They accepted their trophy and posed for pictures.

"I hope you had fun racing," Lightning said, "because I had a great time."

Ramone smiled. "I did," he said. "After all, I had the best teammate!"

Snow Day

Early one morning, Mater awoke to a wonderful surprise. The town of Radiator Springs was completely covered in snow!

"Woo-hoo! Snow day!" he yelled as he threw on his favorite winter hat and drove into town.

Mater was always happy on the first snowfall of the season. But this time it was different. Now his best friend Lightning McQueen was living in Radiator Springs. "I'm going to show Lightning how to *really* have some winter fun!" he exclaimed.

Everyone in town was busy cleaning up the snow. Sheriff and Red had just finished clearing Main Street. The other cars were making sure customers could get into their shops. As Mater pulled into Flo's V8 Café, he saw Lightning. The race car had snow tires on so he wouldn't slip and slide.

"Hey buddy," said Mater, "looks like you're ready to go play in the snow."

"That's right, Mater," replied Lightning. "Let's hit the slopes!"

Mater and Lightning drove around the corner and saw their friend Ramone. He had just finished giving himself a new paint job. He had white snowflakes on his hood and doors, over an icy shade of blue. Lightning and Mater were impressed!

"Nice paint job, Ramone!" said Lightning. "Can you give me a new look, too?"

"Sure!" the hot rod replied. "I can add some snowflakes that will go great with your shade of red."

Ramone took Lightning and Mater over to his shop and got to work. Soon Lightning was sporting some snowflakes. As soon as Ramone had finished painting, Lightning rushed over to a mirror.

"How do you like your new 'snowstyle'?" asked Ramone.

"It's great!" said Lightning. "Thanks, Ramone!"

"Now it's time to go dashing through the snow!" Mater said. The two friends roared off.

Lightning and Mater rolled through the snow until they reached the top of the largest hill in town.

"Race you to the bottom!" said Mater. "Last one down has a rusty crankshaft!"

"You're on!" replied Lightning. "On your mark, get set . . . go!"

Lightning was fast, but Mater took the lead. He laughed as he plowed through the snow. Lightning tried to pass him on the right. Mater blocked him. Then Lightning tried to pass him on the left, but Mater swerved in front of him.

"*Snow* way, Lightning!" Mater chuckled. "Try again!"

Halfway down the hill, one of Mater's wheels hit a patch of ice. The tow truck spun around and around until he was driving backward.

"Watch out below!" he cried as he skidded and crashed into a huge pile of snow.

"You win," said Lightning as he rolled to a stop.

After helping Mater out of the snowbank, Lightning led him over to a frozen lake. Sarge was checking the ice to make sure it wouldn't crack if the cars skated on it.

"It looks okay to me," said Lightning.

"Better safe than sorry," replied Sarge as he moved slowly across the ice. Finally, he called out, "All clear!"

It was time to skate!

Lightning watched Sally glide along the ice. She was a great skater.

I can do that, he said to himself as he tried some of her moves. But he didn't do so well. He slipped and spun around in circles until he was dizzy.

"You may know a lot about racing," Sally said with a laugh, "but you still have a few things to learn about ice-skating!" She showed off her snow tires, which were helping her stay on track.

Meanwhile, Ramone and Flo were gliding around the ice.

"Slow and low is the way to go, even on the ice and snow," said Ramone.

Luigi and Guido didn't agree. They raced each other across the lake until they were both out of breath. That's when Mater had a great idea for a game. He used his hook and cable to take Luigi and Guido for a spin!

"*Toot-toot*! All aboard the Mater Express!" he yelled as he slowly began to pull his friends faster and faster across the ice.

"We've got speed limits on the ice, too," said Sheriff. "Slow down before someone gets hurt."

"You betcha!" replied Mater as he pulled Guido and Luigi in a wide loop around Sally and Lightning.

"That looks like fun," said Sally.

"Yeah," said Lightning. "If you can keep your wheels under you." He was still trying to learn to skate.

Everyone was having a wonderful time except for Lizzie. She didn't really like the cold weather.

"This ice is freezing!" she said. "I can't feel the treads on my tires anymore!"

"Come take a break by the fire," suggested Fillmore. "It's nice and warm over here."

Just as the cars finished skating, the snow began to fall again. Some of the cars started to head back home, but Mater had a better idea.

"Let's catch snowflakes on our tongues!" he said.

Lightning stuck out his tongue like Mater. They drove around trying to catch the falling snow. Before long, Red and Sally joined them!

"This is so much fun!" exclaimed Sally.

Meanwhile, Luigi and Guido were getting ready for a snowball fight. They waited behind a tree with a huge pile. Soon, they saw some of their friends coming down the road.

Guido smiled at Luigi. Then he turned back to the road and launched snowballs at Mater and Lightning.

"Watch out, Mater!" Lightning yelled as he ducked for cover. Mater drove in reverse. He dodged one snowball, then hid behind a tree. But when he peeked out to check if the coast was clear, he saw Guido tossing five snowballs his way.

"Oww! Ow! Ow! Ow!" said Mater as the snowballs hit his roof. "Now that's gonna leave a mark!"

A little while later, the cars rolled back into town. The sun was beginning to set. One by one, the neon lights from the storefronts flickered on, lighting up the sky. Everyone stopped to enjoy the beautiful colors that bounced off the clean white snow.

"The town looks great!" said Sally. "It really is a winter wonderland!"

"Sure is!" said Lightning. "Would you like to take a cruise with me down Main Street?" he asked.

"I'd love to!" replied Sally.

Just then, Mater pulled up beside them.

"Did you have a good snow day, Lightning?" asked Mater.

"Honestly," said Lightning, "I didn't have as much fun as I'm going to have tomorrow when I zip past you on that snowy hill!"

"You better have a light breakfast," joked Mater, " 'cause you'll be eating lots of snow while you're trying to catch up to me!"

"You're on!" Lightning said with a smile.

After a long day of playing in the snow, all of the cars headed over to Flo's.

"There's nothing better than a warm sip on a cold winter night," said Lightning.

"You're wrong, buddy," replied Mater. "It's better to have friends to share a can after a long day of fun!"

"You got that right," replied Flo. "Now drink up before it gets cold!"

Kicking Up Dust

Lightning McQueen and his friends were busy practicing. Chick Hicks had challenged Lightning to a relay race. But this time, the cars wouldn't be driving on a track. They would be racing through the desert. Lightning needed a partner who could handle the rough course.

The other Radiator Springs cars were doing their best, but racing off-road was hard. Sarge watched as Ramone tried to climb a rocky hill. Mater had to help Fillmore out of a silt bed.

"You cars are hopeless!" Sarge said. "Don't you know how to drive off-road?"

That gave Lightning an idea. "Maybe you should be my partner, Sarge," he said. "You can show me what you know about driving when the ground is rough."

"I've never raced before," Sarge replied.

"Then we can teach each other!" Lightning said.

"All right, soldier," Sarge agreed. "Let's get training."

Meanwhile, Chick Hicks had chosen his partner, too. El Machismo was a big truck. Off-road racing was his specialty. He had tough tires and a special set of fog lights so he could see anything in his path.

El Machismo climbed hills with ease. He sped over bumpy rocks without even noticing them. He kicked up dust right and left.

"Finally," Chick said. "Here is a partner who can help me beat Lightning McQueen once and for all!"

"Yeah!" agreed El Machismo. "We'll crush those wimpy little cars!" He roared his engine.

Chick chuckled. "Of course, I'll be ready with a few of my usual tricks as well," he said. "Just in case."

"You won't need them!" El Machismo called out as he jumped over a giant cactus.

"We'll see," Chick said. He was amazed at the truck's skills. But he didn't want to take any chances.

The next morning Lightning and Sarge were hard at work. Sarge taught Lightning about driving off-road. The race car tried going through lakes, up rocky hills, and around desert plants.

The hills were a problem. Lightning couldn't get a grip on the loose rocks with his tires!

"We'll make sure you have the right tires for the race, soldier!" Sarge said.

Then, Lightning showed Sarge what it was like to race against Chick Hicks. He set up an obstacle course filled with the dirty tricks Chick liked to play.

"When you race against Chick Hicks, the most important thing is to expect the unexpected," Lightning said.

By the end of the day, Sarge and Lightning both felt ready for the big race. But Sarge had one more lesson to teach the race car.

The two cars drove up to a cliff that looked out over the desert. Lightning was sure he'd be able to get around the rocks and catci.

"There's one more thing you have to know how to handle," Sarge said. "Silt."

"Silt?" Lightning asked. "You mean loose dirt?"

"Affirmative," Sarge replied. "It doesn't sound like much, but if you hit a patch of silt the wrong way, you'll be stuck spinning your wheels in a cloud of dust."

Sarge told Lightning what to do. "Make sure you're in the lead. When the dust starts flying, keep driving no matter how much you want to stop. Got it?"

"Yes, sir!" Lightning said.

Just before the race, Lightning and Sarge went to Luigi's Casa Della Tires. Guido put brand-new off-road tires on both cars. Now Lightning would have no trouble with the rocky hills!

The race car also had a set of fog lights installed on his roof. Sarge wanted him to be ready for anything.

When they pulled up to the off-road course, they saw El Machismo.

"Bow down to the tower of power!" the truck roared.

Sarge scoffed. "That tower of metal is going to learn to lose today," he said.

Sarge would be up against Chick during the first part of the race. He rolled up to the starting line. Chick was already there, revving his engine.

Chick looked at Sarge and laughed. "Rookie!" he said.

Sarge glared at Chick. "Civilian," he replied.

Then the green flag waved. The race was on!

Sarge and Chick took off. Chick had a lot more racing experience, but Sarge kept up with him.

After a bumpy stretch of terrain, Chick pulled ahead. Suddenly, Chick dumped a bunch of bolts right in front of Sarge!

Sarge swerved right, then left. He knew how to handle bumpy roads! And his new off-road tires were too tough for the bolts to damage. Sarge sped toward the pit stop, where Lightning was waiting to begin his part of the race.

Chick was so busy watching Sarge dodge the bolts, he didn't see what was right in front of him. He crashed into a huge cactus.

"Ouch!" Chick cried. He pulled himself off the prickly plant and headed for the pit stop.

El Machismo was waiting.

"You make sure you beat Lightning McQueen!" Chick yelled as his pit crew tried to remove the needles from his tires.

"No problem!" El Machismo said. He roared off. Lightning already had a head start!

El Machismo chased after Lightning. He caught up to the race car on a rickety old bridge that crossed over the river.

Uh-oh, Lightning thought. That giant truck is tougher than I thought!

He watched El Machismo race up a hill and jump off, soaring high over Lightning's head.

Lightning knew he had to race even harder! If he didn't hit the silt beds first, he didn't stand a chance.

As the two cars reached a narrow path, Lightning put on a burst of speed. He cut in front of El Machismo and took the lead again.

Lightning looked ahead. He could see a large section of dusty dirt.

"Silt!" he said. This was it! Sarge had told him exactly what to do.

Lightning hit the loose dirt. Dust flew up all around him. "Whoa!" he yelled. "I can't see a thing!" He wanted to slow down or stop. But Sarge had told him to keep going.

Lightning revved his engine and drove through the silt as fast as he could.

When Lightning got through it, he could see the finish line in the distance. El Machismo was nowhere in sight.

"Ha!" Lightning exclaimed. "Sarge was right. I kicked up so much dust that that big truck is lost!"

Chick saw what happened and tried to change the race sign.
But Lightning had crossed the finish line!

Suddenly, he heard El Machismo coughing. "That race car,"
the truck said. "He kicked up so much dust, I—*ahh-choo*!"

Chick frowned. Lightning had beaten him again.

Lightning and Sarge drove to the podium and accepted their trophy.

"Not bad for your first race, right, Sarge?" Lightning said.

"Affirmative, soldier," Sarge replied. "Racing off-road is something I'd do again any day."

Lightning was happy to hear that. He couldn't wait to go driving off-road with Sarge again!

Team Red

One afternoon, Sheriff called all the cars in Radiator Springs together for an important meeting.

"We've had a lot of extra cars in town lately," he said. "Red here needs some help making sure everyone stays safe. Fires are dangerous!"

"Can I volunteer?" asked Lightning McQueen. The race car was eager to help.

Soon, other cars had offered to pitch in

Sarge told the cars they would have to try out for the job.

"Okay, everybody," he said, "let's see what you can do!"

Sarge led the cars who wanted to volunteer over to a brass bell. "The first step to fire safety is sounding the alarm," he said. "When you hear the bell, you should gather at the firehouse to get your instructions."

Red, the shy fire engine, nodded firmly. He was glad Sarge was helping him train the volunteers.

Fillmore offered to go first. "I can ring the bell," he said. He drove very slowly up to the stand.

"That won't work!" Sarge yelled. "This is an emergency! The bell ringer has to move like—"

"Like Lightning!" finished the race car. He zoomed over to the bell.

But he couldn't slow down in time. He knocked into the stand with his back wheel. *BRIIIINNNG!* The bell clanged as it flew off the stand.

"I'll tell Sheriff we need a new bell," Doc Hudson said to Sarge.

For the next drill, Red and Sarge asked Luigi and Guido to raise a ladder up to the roof of the firehouse.

"Guido will-a do that," Luigi said.

The little forklift zipped over to the ladder. He picked it up and started to raise it toward the firehouse.

"Up, up, up-a she goes!" Luigi crowed.

The ladder was heavy, and it was much too big for the forklift to handle. Guido struggled to keep his grip on it. Suddenly, it slipped!

"And down, down, down-a she comes!" Luigi cried.

The ladder fell toward Sarge. He zoomed out of the way just in time. "That was close!"

For the final test, Red wanted to see the cars work a fire hydrant and hose.

Ramone took charge of the hydrant. Mater offered to untangle the hose.

The hot rod quickly got the cover off the hydrant.

Water gushed out and showered Sarge.

"No, no, no!" Sarge yelled. "You're not supposed to turn on the water until the hose is hooked up."

Ramone and Lightning looked at Mater. Instead of untangling the hose, Mater had gotten himself tangled in it!

Red chose all the cars who tried out to be part of his team. He knew they still had a lot to learn about fire safety. But he was willing to teach them.

The volunteers practiced and practiced. Mater still had a little trouble with the hose. One time he left a knot in the middle, which meant the water couldn't get through. And sometimes Lightning still zoomed past the bell.

But they worked hard, and Red was sure they would be ready when it was time to fight their first real fire.

One afternoon, Red's team got a big surprise. They had been chosen to lead the annual Radiator Springs Day parade.

Ramone offered to give the team new paint jobs.

Red got a fresh coat of red paint. He knew it would shine in the sunlight.

Lightning decided to change his look completely. He asked Ramone to paint him bright yellow. Then Ramone painted a red fire-team logo on his side.

Luigi asked for the same logo. "Look-a at me!" he exclaimed. "Just like a real race car!"

He was so excited, he offered the whole team new tires.

Guido put on Lightning's new tires in two-and-a-half seconds, flat. He was the fastest tire changer around.

"Now we are-a ready for the parade," Luigi said.

The next morning, Red was on Main Street waiting for the rest of his team. Suddenly, the fire engine saw a cloud of smoke. He raced to the firehouse to ring the bell.

Lightning McQueen was the first to arrive. "Red, what's going

on?" he asked.

"Fire!" Red said.

Lightning looked down Main Street at the smoke. "Let's go!" he said.

Red and Lightning picked up the other volunteers along the way. Luigi, Guido, and Ramone were ready to fight their first fire!

"Hey," Lightning said, "where's Mater?"

The other cars looked at each other. No one had seen the tow truck that morning.

"Maybe he's-a waiting for us," Luigi said.

"That must be it," Lightning agreed. The cars drove at top speed toward the cloud of smoke.

When they got close enough, Guido and Luigi helped Lightning set up the hose. Then Lightning turned on the water.

Guido and Red surrounded the fire, spraying water on it from both sides. The smoke cleared, and they saw Mater.

Lightning gasped. "What are you doing here?"

Mater spit the water out. "I saw some smoke, so I came out here to see what the trouble was," he said. "But the fire got out of control before I could call for help, and I couldn't see through the smoke."

Ramone turned off the fire hydrant. "You should never go near a fire on your own. It's too dangerous. That's why we have a fire department."

"That's right!" Lightning agreed. He turned to Red and the rest of the volunteers. "We did it, guys! We put out our first fire!"

Just then, Lizzie came driving down the street, a trail of confetti behind her. "Here you are!" she said. "Happy Radiator Springs Day, everyone!"

Red and his team got into position. They were ready to lead the parade.

Red and his team drove down Main Street as music played and the other cars cheered.

"Good job, Team Red!" Sarge called out as the volunteer firefighters drove by.

The team smiled. All of their hard work had paid off. They hoped they wouldn't have to fight many more fires. But now they knew that if an alarm sounded, they would be ready.

The Big Show

Life in Radiator Springs was nice and easy for Lightning McQueen. He drove slowly down Main Street, taking in the sights and sounds of the town.

The race car smiled wide as he pulled into Tow Mater Towing and Salvage. His friend Mater grinned and drove over beside him.

"Hey there, buddy," the tow truck said. "Aren't you a sight for sore eyes!"

"I'm in the mood for a little fun today, Mater," Lightning said. What do you say we come up with something amazing to do?"

Mater thought for a moment. "Want to go tractor tipping?" he asked.

"Nah. We did that last week," Lightning said.

"I know!" Mater grinned. "I can race you backward to the firehouse!"

Lightning sighed. "That wouldn't be bad, but . . . I was hoping for something, well, bigger."

"Bigger," Mater repeated, nodding. "Bigger . . . bigger . . ."

They soon met some of the other cars over by the tire shop. As they were talking Sally drove past, gleaming in the sunshine. She beeped hello.

"Hi, Sally! Bye, Sally!" Mater yelled.

Lightning flashed his lucky lightning-bolt sticker at her. *"Ka-ch*—Hey, what's her hurry? Oh, I know. I bet she's off to solve another legal crisis." Not only was Sally the prettiest car Lightning had ever seen, she was one of the smartest.

"Aw, did you see the way she shined her mirrors at you? That was just plum showing off," Mater said. "But, shoot, I'd be a show-off too if I was all pretty and clean like she is."

"You think she was showing off? For me?" Lightning asked.

"'Course I do," Mater replied. "A car like Sally was made for the spotlight."

Lightning smiled. "Mater! That's it. You're a genius!"

"I am?" The tow truck blinked.

We'll round up everyone and have a good old-fashioned car show tonight!" Lightning exclaimed.

Mater grinned. "You always have the best ideas, buddy."

"Not without some inspiration from my best friend!" Lightning and Mater drove over to Flo's V8 Café for a breakfast fill-up.

The tow truck looked around. "Maybe Flo would let us have the show here?"

"Let's ask her!" Lightning said.

When Flo heard their idea, she lit up with excitement. "Oh, boy! That's the best idea I've heard in a long time!" Flo had been a Motorama girl years ago before she came to Radiator Springs. She promised to give tips to any cars that wanted them. "After all, my days on the circuit taught me a lot about this kind of thing."

Lightning and Mater thanked Flo and hurried off to spread the word.

"This news is-a so good-a it makes me the happiest car in the world!" Luigi exclaimed. "It will mean big-a business for Casa Della Tires!"

Guido nodded excitedly.

Ramone was happy, too. "My appointment book's already filling up," he said as Mater and Lightning passed by Ramone's House of Body Art. "Good thing I just got a shipment of new paint colors."

"*Whee-hoo!* Folks sure do move fast," Mater said as they watched two cars dash into Fillmore's for some organic fuel and tie-dyed mud flaps.

"That's what I'm always telling you, Mater," Lightning said. "When it comes to having fun, it's all about . . . speed!"

The race car sped off toward the Wheel Well to find Sally. He couldn't wait to tell her about the show! He knew she would be thrilled.

"That sounds wonderful," Sally said when Lightning told her about the show. She was busy scheduling day trips for the customers at the Wheel Well. Since the motel had reopened, she spent all her free time making sure that visitors were happy.

"Everyone's really excited," Lightning said.

Sally smiled. "What a great way to boost everyone's spirits!"

They drove back into town. The businesses on Main Street were bustling with customers. Sarge waved as they drove past his army surplus store. "Make sure to get in line early for a car wash!" he called. "I waited for over an hour!"

"Luigi, would you have time to give me two new tires?" Sally asked as she pulled up to the tire shop. "Mine are getting a little worn down."

"For you, Miss Sally, anything!" Luigi exclaimed, waving her in. Lightning said good-bye and sped over to Ramone's. He was going to get some new lightning bolts!

After Sally got her new tires, she headed for the car wash. She noticed a little gray car pulled over to the side of the street with his flashers on. He looked lost.

"Hi there. My name's Sally," she said, pulling up alongside him. "Do you need some help?"

"I'm Marty," the car said. "Where am I?"

"You're in Radiator Springs," Sally said proudly. "And you've arrived just in time for our first annual car show. It's tonight!"

The car looked nervous. "I'm afraid I can't stay around for a car show. I just got off the Interstate to get some gasoline."

"Come with me," Sally said, leading the way. "Flo's V8 Café has just what you need."

"Hey, Sally! Who's your new friend?" Mater called as they drove past. He and Fillmore were on the way to get their tires rotated.

"Marty. He's just passing through," Sally explained.

As Marty's tank was filling up at Flo's, Sally studied a map. "You need to drive through Ornament Valley and continue on for about twenty miles," she said.

"Twenty miles?" Marty looked stressed. "I'm already late for a meeting!"

"There is a shortcut," Sally said. "But it will take you through some bumpy territory." She wasn't sure the frazzled car was up to the challenge.

Marty took a big gulp of gasoline. "Do you think you'd be able to show me?"

"Well . . ." Sally broke off as Lightning zoomed up.

"Check this out!" He showed off his new lightning bolts. "Cars from far and wide have heard about our show. Cool, huh?"

Sally laughed. "Really cool." She introduced Marty to Lightning. "He is in a hurry, and I'm trying to help him."

"Sally's the best map reader in town," Lightning said. "She'll help you get wherever you need to go."

"So, can you show me the way?" Marty asked again.

"But what about the car show?" Lightning cried.

"If we leave now I'll be back in plenty of time," Sally declared.

"Let me take him," Lightning offered. "I don't want you to miss the show."

But Sally knew Lightning would be too fast for Marty to follow.

"I know these roads better than anyone," Sally said. "I'll be back before you know it!"

Lightning waved good-bye as Sally and Marty set off. "Come back and visit!" he said.

Sally and Marty drove to Ornament Valley. When they reached the shortcut, Sally slowed down. The road wasn't well-marked. If Marty made a wrong turn, he'd be even more lost.

She took a deep breath. "This way," she said, turning onto the dusty old mountain road.

When they reached the Interstate, Marty gave Sally a grateful beep good-bye. Sally sped back toward Radiator Springs.

She made it in time for the car show . . . but she was covered with dust, and one of her tires was quickly losing air!

Sally was about to turn around when Flo spotted her. "You're just in time!" she exclaimed.

"I think it's too late," Sally replied as she watched all the shiny cars drive past.

"It's never too late!" Lightning zoomed up with Red and Luigi. In minutes, the fire engine had hosed off the dust and Luigi had fitted her with a new tire.

"You guys are the best!" Sally declared. She drove up to the stage for her turn in the spotlight.

"Sally, you're the prettiest car here!" Mater shouted.

The sports car beamed. "Thanks, Mater," she said, letting the spotlight shine on her. She'd never felt like such a star.

Mater's Secret Mission

In the middle of the ocean, a British secret agent named Finn McMissile climbed up the side of an oil rig. He turned on his listening device and started to look around. Soon he saw a group of cars on a lower deck, including one named Grem and another called Acer.

Suddenly, a new car appeared. Finn's computer identified the car as a criminal named Professor Z. He and the other cars on the rig were up to no good.

Finn took as many photos as he could.

Before Finn could leave the rig, the professor spotted him. "Get him!" he yelled.

Grem, Acer, and the others chased Finn across the oil rig and onto a crane. Finn dropped a bunch of oil drums onto the other cars and climbed up to the rig's helicopter pad. But there was nowhere else to go!

Finn jumped overboard and pretended to sink, but secretly he turned into a submarine and got to safety.

"Wonderful!" the professor said. "Now no one can stop us!"

Back in Radiator Springs, Lightning McQueen was having dinner with Sally. He was done racing for the season and glad to have lots of time off.

Mater was their waiter. While he was getting their drinks, Mater saw Sir Miles Axlerod on TV. Axlerod said he had created a new fuel called Allinol that could be used instead of gasoline.

"What do you think of that?" Sarge asked Fillmore.

Fillmore scoffed. "Once Big Oil, always Big Oil, man," he said.

A car named Francesco appeared on the screen. He was going to race in Axlerod's World Grand Prix. The TV host asked him why Lightning wasn't racing. "He is afraid of Francesco!" the race car replied.

Soon Mater had called in to the show. "Lightning could beat you anytime!" he said. When Francesco began to make fun of Mater, Lightning got on the phone and said he would enter the race.

Lightning decided to take Mater and the rest of the Radiator Springs gang to the World Grand Prix. They would act as his crew. Before the first race in Tokyo, Axlerod threw a huge party.

Lightning started talking to some of the other race cars. But Mater didn't know what to do. He saw something that looked like pistachio ice cream. The chef tried to tell him that it was spicy wasabi, but Mater took a big scoop anyway.

When Mater tasted the wasabi, he screamed! He started driving all around, trying to find some water. Finally, he stopped. Everyone was looking at him—and the pool of oil on the floor.

Mater went to the restroom to clean himself up. "I never leak oil," he told himself, confused.

While Mater was in the stall, an American secret agent named Rod "Torque" Redline came into the bathroom. He had a device with a tracker so that his British partners could find him. But two bad cars named Grem and Acer appeared and started to fight with Torque.

When Mater came out, Torque stuck his tracker and some secret information to the tow truck just before he left.

Outside the bathroom, British spy car Holley Shiftwell was waiting. She detected the tracker and thought Mater was a secret agent!

"Let's talk tomorrow at the races," she said to him.

The next day, Mater went to the race track with Lightning and the rest of his friends. He thought he had a date with Holley.

The race began. Mater talked to Lightning over a radio and told him where to go. Lightning was winning!

High above the race track, Professor Z had other plans. He had sabotaged the Allinol fuel that the racers were using. When Grem and Acer zapped a car with a special camera, it did something to the fuel that made the engine burst into flames!

Holley was watching the race, too. She spotted Mater and started talking to him over the radio, telling him how to find her. "Go outside," she said.

"Go outside?" Mater repeated.

Lightning thought Mater was talking to him over the radio. He moved to the outside of the track. Francesco sped past him and over the finish line. Mater tried to explain, but Lightning was furious.

"I don't need your help!" Lightning said.

Mater was sad that he let his best friend down. He decided to fly back to Radiator Springs. But Finn was at the airport waiting for him.

The secret agent introduced himself. "Finn McMissile, British Intelligence," he said.

"Tow Mater," Mater replied. "Average intelligence."

Finn noticed that Grem and Acer were chasing them. He fended them off while Mater towed Finn toward a plane. Mater didn't even realize they were being chased!

Finn and Holley still thought Mater was a spy and that he acted silly so no one would know.

Holley took the tracking device off Mater and dropped it into the plane's computer. A photo popped up. Torque, the American agent, had taken it, but Holley and Finn thought Mater had. "What is it?" Finn asked him.

Mater hadn't taken the picture, but he knew a bad engine when he saw one. He told Finn and Holley that it was one of the worst gas-guzzling engines ever made and it had special bolts. But he had no idea whose engine it was.

The next race in the World Grand Prix was in Italy, so the Radiator Springs gang stayed with Luigi's Uncle Topolino. Lightning missed Mater and wished he hadn't gotten angry.

Uncle Topolino told him it was important to stand by friends. Lightning thought about that.

Meanwhile, Mater and the spies were on their way to Italy, too. Holley gave Mater a disguise. She also gave him a voice-activated defense system. The plan was for Mater to sneak into a meeting to find out what was going on with the race.

With his disguise, Mater fit right in with all the other cars at the meeting.

Professor Z came in. He introduced his boss, who told the cars that once Allinol was proven dangerous, cars would go back to gas. That would help all of them gain power and become rich.

Meanwhile, at the race, Lightning crossed the finish line just before there was a big pile up.

Sir Axlerod made an announcement: the cars would not use Allinol in the final race. But Lightning decided to use the special fuel anyway, because Fillmore had told him it was safe. "I didn't stand by a friend recently," he said to the press. "I'm not making the same mistake again."

The professor was watching. His boss had told him that Lightning was a problem he'd need to take care of.

Mater left to warn Lightning, but the professor had the others catch him. Before Mater knew it, he'd been knocked out.

When Mater woke up, he was in London, site of the final race. He was also trapped inside a clock called Big Bentley. He, Finn, and Holley were all being held prisoner by Grem and Acer. The two bad cars had their special camera. They knew Lightning was running on Allinol and they were waiting to zap him.

When they tried, luckily nothing happened. Mater was so relieved.

"Time for the backup plan," Grem said. "We planted a bomb in Lightning's pit!" The two bad cars left, laughing.

"Dadgum!" Mater exclaimed. He used his spy gear to escape. He was almost to Lightning's pit when Finn and Holley broke free and realized that Mater was carrying the bomb.

CARS STORYBOOK COLLECTION

"Mater!" Finn yelled through the radio. "The bomb is on you! They put it there when we were knocked out!"

Mater was close to Lightning, but when he heard that, he drove the other way. Lightning chased him and grabbed his tow hook. He wanted to apologize.

Mater activated his defense system, and his rockets propelled the two friends away so the professor couldn't set off the bomb.

Holley and Finn captured Professor Z and brought him to Mater. But the professor couldn't do anything. Only his mysterious boss could turn off the bomb.

Guido tried to take the bomb off Mater. But none of the wrenches fit the bolts.

"I get it!" Mater cried. He and Lightning used rocket launchers and a parachute and went to Axlerod, who was with the Queen. The timer on Mater's bomb was counting down. Just as it was about to go off, Axlerod called out, "Deactivate!" The timer stopped.

Mater explained that Axlerod had made the puddle of oil at the party in Tokyo. Old British engines leaked oil, and Torque's photograph had shown an old British engine with Whitworth bolts, just like the ones that had attached the bomb to Mater.

It turned out that Axlerod secretly owned oil rigs, and wanted cars to buy gasoline so he could get rich. So he made sure no one trusted alternative fuel.

"But why didn't I explode?" Lightning asked. "I was running on Allinol, too."

Everyone looked at Fillmore. "If you're saying I switched out the Allinol for my homemade fuel, you're wrong." He pointed to Sarge. "It was him."

"Once Big Oil, always Big Oil," Sarge said. "Man."

Soon the gang was back in Radiator Springs. The final race was to be held there. Mater was thrilled to be back home with his best friend.